CLARKSON POTTER

Copyright © 2012, 2017 by R.J. Palacio

All rights reserved.

Published in the United States by Clarkson
Potter/Publishers, an imprint of the Crown
Publishing Group, a division of Penguin Random
House LLC, New York

crownpublishing.com
clarksonpotter.com

CLARKSON POTTER is a trademark and
POTTER with colophon is a registered
trademark of Penguin Random House LLC

Inspired by *Wonder* by R.J. Palacio, copyright
© 2012, 2017 by R.J. Palacio.

Published by Alfred A. Knopf, an imprint of
Random House Children's Books, a division
of Penguin Random House LLC, New York

Art by Tad Carpenter and Vaughn Fender
Art and logo type copyright © 2012, 2017 by
R.J. Palacio and Random House Children's Books

ISBN 978-1-5247-5941-4

Printed in China

.

 CLARKSON POTTER

Copyright © 2012, 2017 by R.J. Palacio

All rights reserved.

Published in the United States by Clarkson
Potter/Publishers, an imprint of the Crown
Publishing Group, a division of Penguin Random
House LLC, New York

crownpublishing.com
clarksonpotter.com

CLARKSON POTTER is a trademark and
POTTER with colophon is a registered
trademark of Penguin Random House LLC

Inspired by *Wonder* by R.J. Palacio, copyright
© 2012, 2017 by R.J. Palacio.

Published by Alfred A. Knopf, an imprint of
Random House Children's Books, a division
of Penguin Random House LLC, New York

Art by Tad Carpenter and Vaughn Fender
Art and logo type copyright © 2012, 2017 by
R.J. Palacio and Random House Children's Books

ISBN 978-1-5247-5941-4

Printed in China

CLARKSON POTTER

Published in the United States by Clarkson
Potter/Publishers, an imprint of the Crown
Publishing Group, a division of Penguin Random
House LLC, New York

crownpublishing.com
clarksonpotter.com

CLARKSON POTTER is a trademark and
POTTER with colophon is a registered
trademark of Penguin Random House LLC

Inspired by *Wonder* by R.J. Palacio, copyright
© 2012, 2017 by R.J. Palacio.

Published by Alfred A. Knopf, an imprint of
Random House Children's Books, a division
of Penguin Random House LLC, New York

Art by Tad Carpenter and Vaughn Fender
Art and logo type copyright © 2012, 2017 by
R.J. Palacio and Random House Children's Books

ISBN 978-1-5247-5941-4

Printed in China

 CLARKSON POTTER

Copyright © 2012, 2017 by R.J. Palacio

All rights reserved.

Published in the United States by Clarkson
Potter/Publishers, an imprint of the Crown
Publishing Group, a division of Penguin Random
House LLC, New York

crownpublishing.com
clarksonpotter.com

CLARKSON POTTER is a trademark and
POTTER with colophon is a registered
trademark of Penguin Random House LLC

Inspired by *Wonder* by R.J. Palacio, copyright
© 2012, 2017 by R.J. Palacio.

Published by Alfred A. Knopf, an imprint of
Random House Children's Books, a division
of Penguin Random House LLC, New York

Art by Tad Carpenter and Vaughn Fender
Art and logo type copyright © 2012, 2017 by
R.J. Palacio and Random House Children's Books

ISBN 978-1-5247-5941-4

Printed in China